The
HIGHWAYMAN

HARCOURT BRACE JOVANOVICH, PUBLISHERS

San Diego   *New York*   *London*

The
HIGHWAYMAN

WRITTEN BY
Alfred Noyes

ILLUSTRATED BY
Neil Waldman

HBJ

Artwork based on a sketch created by Bryna Waldman

Requests for permission to make copies of
any part of the work should be mailed to:
Permissions Department,
Harcourt Brace Jovanovich, Publishers,
Orlando, Florida 32887.

Library of Congress Cataloging-in-Publication Data
Noyes, Alfred, 1880–1958.
The highwayman/written by Alfred Noyes;
illustrated by Neil Waldman.
p.   cm.
Summary: An illustrated version of the well-known
poem about the highwayman and his true love,
the innkeeper's daughter.
ISBN 0-15-234340-7
1. Brigands and robbers—Juvenile poetry.   2. Children's poetry,
English.   [1. Robbers and outlaws— Poetry.   2. Narrative poetry,
3. English poetry.]   I. Waldman, Neil, ill.   II. Title.
PR6027.O8H5   1990
821'.912—dc19   89-30805

First edition
A B C D E

The illustrations in this book were done in Prang
watercolors on 140-lb. d'Arches cold-pressed paper.

The display type was set in Goudy Thirty.

The text type was set in Fournier.

Composition by Thompson Type, San Diego, California

Color separations were made by Fine Graphic Arts, Hong Kong.

Printed and bound by South China Printing Co. Ltd., Hong Kong

Production supervision by Warren Wallerstein and Ginger Boyer

Designed by Michael Farmer

To my beloved sister, Bryna,
whose pencil sketches helped me to
formulate the character of Bess.

—N. W.

PART I

The wind was a torrent of darkness among the gusty trees,
The moon was a ghostly galleon tossed upon cloudy seas,
The road was a ribbon of moonlight over the purple moor,
And the highwayman came riding—
      Riding—riding—
The highwayman came riding, up to the old inn-door.

He'd a French cocked-hat on his forehead, a bunch of lace at his chin,
A coat of the claret velvet, and breeches of brown doe-skin;
They fitted with never a wrinkle; his boots were up to the thigh!
And he rode with a jeweled twinkle,
      His pistol butts a-twinkle,
His rapier hilt a-twinkle, under the jeweled sky.

Over the cobbles he clattered and clashed in the dark inn-yard,
And he tapped with his whip on the shutters, but all was locked
   and barred;
He whistled a tune to the window, and who should be waiting there
But the landlord's black-eyed daughter,
       Bess, the landlord's daughter,
Plaiting a dark red love-knot into her long black hair.

And dark in the dark old inn-yard a stable-wicket creaked
Where Tim the ostler listened; his face was white and peaked;
His eyes were hollows of madness, his hair like moldy hay,
But he loved the landlord's daughter,
        The landlord's red-lipped daughter,
Dumb as a dog he listened, and he heard the robber say—

"One kiss, my bonny sweetheart, I'm after a prize tonight,
But I shall be back with the yellow gold before the morning light;
Yet, if they press me sharply, and harry me through the day,
Then look for me by moonlight,
        Watch for me by moonlight,
I'll come to thee by moonlight, though hell should bar the way."

He rose upright in the stirrups; he scarce could reach her hand,
But she loosened her hair i' the casement! His face burned like
  a brand
As the black cascade of perfume came tumbling over his breast;
And he kissed its waves in the moonlight,
        (Oh, sweet black waves in the moonlight!)
Then he tugged at his rein in the moonlight, and galloped away to
  the West.

PART II

He did not come in the dawning; he did not come at noon;
And out o' the tawny sunset, before the rise o' the moon,
When the road was a gypsy's ribbon, looping the purple moor,
A red-coat troop came marching—
        Marching—marching—
King George's men came marching, up to the old inn-door.

They said no word to the landlord, they drank his ale instead,
But they gagged his daughter and bound her to the foot of her
  narrow bed;
Two of them knelt at her casement, with muskets at their side!
There was death at every window;
        And hell at one dark window;
For Bess could see, through her casement, the road that he
  would ride.

They had tied her up to attention, with many a sniggering jest;
They had bound a musket beside her, with the barrel beneath
    her breast!
"Now keep good watch!" and they kissed her. She heard the dead
    man say—
Look for me by moonlight;
      Watch for me by moonlight;
I'll come to thee by moonlight, though hell should bar the way!

She twisted her hands behind her; but all the knots held good!
She writhed her hands till her fingers were wet with sweat or blood!
They stretched and strained in the darkness, and the hours crawled by
   like years,
Till now, on the stroke of midnight,
      Cold, on the stroke of midnight,
The tip of one finger touched it! The trigger at least was hers!

The tip of one finger touched it; she strove no more for the rest!
Up, she stood up to attention, with the barrel beneath her breast,
She would not risk their hearing: she would not strive again;
For the road lay bare in the moonlight;
      Blank and bare in the moonlight;
And the blood of her veins in the moonlight throbbed to her
   love's refrain.

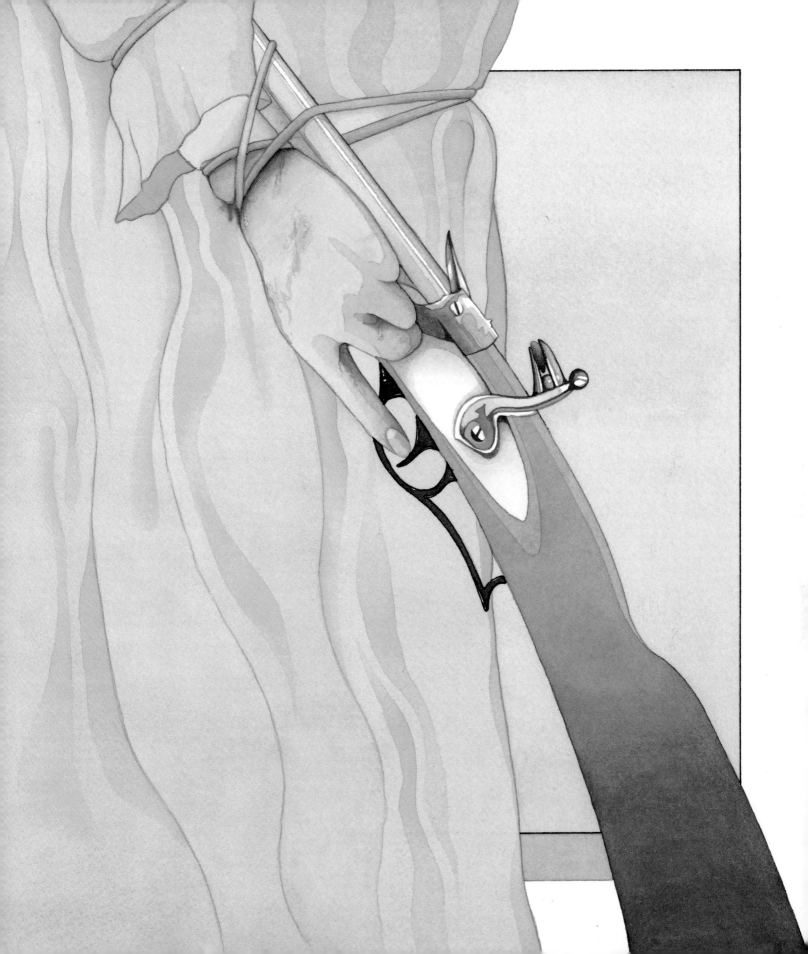

Tlot-tlot; tlot-tlot! Had they heard it? The horse-hoofs ringing clear;
Tlot-tlot, tlot-tlot, in the distance? Were they deaf that they did
   not hear?
Down the ribbon of moonlight, over the brow of the hill,
The highwayman came riding,
      Riding, riding!
The red-coats looked to the priming! She stood up, straight and still!

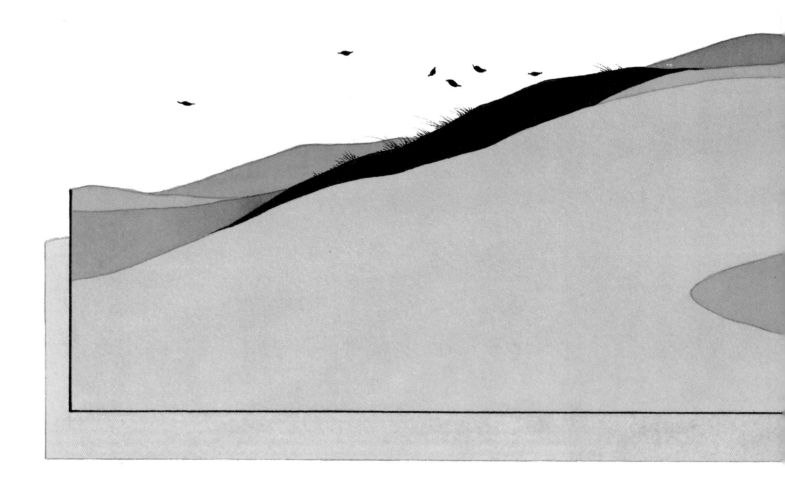

Tlot-tlot, in the frosty silence! *Tlot-tlot,* in the echoing night!
Nearer he came and nearer! Her face was like a light!
Her eyes grew wide for a moment; she drew one last deep breath,
Then her finger moved in the moonlight,
      Her musket shattered the moonlight,
Shattered her breast in the moonlight and warned him—with
   her death.

He turned; he spurred to the westward; he did not know who stood
Bowed, with her head o'er the musket, drenched with her own
  red blood!
Not till the dawn he heard it, his face grew gray to hear
How Bess, the landlord's daughter,
      The landlord's black-eyed daughter,
Had watched for her love in the moonlight, and died in the
  darkness there.

Back he spurred like a madman, shrieking a curse to the sky,
With the white road smoking behind him, and his rapier
brandished high!
Blood-red were his spurs in the golden moon; wine-red was his
velvet coat,
When they shot him down on the highway,
Down like a dog on the highway,
And he lay in his blood on the highway, with a bunch of lace at
his throat.

And still of a winter's night, they say, when the wind is in the trees,
When the moon is a ghostly galleon tossed upon cloudy seas,
When the road is a ribbon of moonlight over the purple moor,
A highwayman comes riding—
        Riding—riding—
A highwayman comes riding, up to the old inn-door.

Over the cobbles he clatters and clangs in the dark inn-yard;
And he taps with his whip on the shutters, but all is locked and barred;
He whistles a tune to the window, and who should be waiting there
        But the landlord's black-eyed daughter
        Bess, the landlord's daughter,
Plaiting a dark red love-knot into her long black hair.